What lives in the sea?

T0337096

Written by Sally Morgan

Illustrated by Rose Wilkinson

Collins

What's in this book?

Listen and say

seal

shark

giant squid

dolphin

whale

"What lives in the sea, Dad?" asks Vicky.

"There are many things," says Dad.

4

"Quick! Look there!" says Dad.

"It's a whale."

"Wow, it's jumping out of the water!"
says Vicky.

Many animals swim in the water. Can you see the shark and the whale?

Starfish cannot swim. They live at the bottom of the sea.

shark

whale

starfish

There are many plants in the sea, too.
These plants are seaweed.

Seaweed is green, brown and red.

seaweed

You often find beaches next to the sea. Some beaches are sandy. Some beaches are rocky.

Waves come up the beach and then they go back again.

Some rocky beaches have rock pools.
Many different animals live in rock pools.
How many arms has the starfish got?

crab

sea anemone

starfish

rock pool

limpet

In some places, there are coral reefs in the sea. Coral reefs are beautiful. They can't grow in cold water. There are lots of colours in a coral reef.

turtle

coral

There are lots of fish in the reef.
How many different fish can you see?
Sharks are fish, too. Sharks eat
smaller fish.

shark

fish

coral reef

Is this a big tree? No, it's seaweed.
It's very long. This seaweed is kelp
and it grows up to the sun.

kelp

seal

Fish swim between the kelp. There are lots of small, orange fish here. There are seals, too. They eat the fish.

The sea is very, very big. Dolphins often jump from the sea. How many dolphins can you see?

dolphin

Many small fish live in the sea. You cannot see them from a boat. These small fish swim together in a school. There are thousands of fish in this school.

a school of fish

Whales are very big animals. Most whales live in a family. This whale is swimming with its baby.

The elephant is the biggest animal that can walk. The blue whale is bigger! It grows to 30 metres long! How many elephants make one blue whale?

The sea goes down and down. It's cold near the bottom and you cannot see the sun. Different fish live here. Look at this giant squid!

fish

giant squid

Giant squids often do terrible things
in stories, but we don't know much
about them. They don't often hurt people.

There's a lot of rubbish in the sea.
You can see bottles, bags, nets and many
different things. The rubbish can hurt the
sea animals.

rubbish

Waves can carry rubbish from our beaches into the sea. Be careful what you put on the beach. Many different animals live in the sea and on the beaches.

We want to keep them safe.

Picture dictionary

Listen and repeat

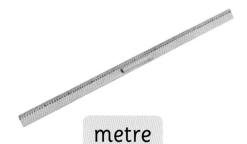

metre

rocky beach

sandy beach

thousand

rubbish

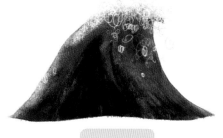

wave

1 Look and say "*Yes*" or "*No*"

Coral reefs are beautiful.

They grow in cold water.

There is no colour in a coral reef.

Many fish live in a coral reef.

There are no sharks in a coral reef.

2 Listen and say

Collins

Published by Collins
An imprint of HarperCollins*Publishers*
Westerhill Road
Bishopbriggs
Glasgow
G64 2QT

HarperCollins*Publishers*
1st Floor, Watermarque Building
Ringsend Road
Dublin 4
Ireland

William Collins' dream of knowledge for all began with the publication of his first book in 1819.

A self-educated mill worker, he not only enriched millions of lives, but also founded a flourishing publishing house. Today, staying true to this spirit, Collins books are packed with inspiration, innovation and practical expertise. They place you at the centre of a world of possibility and give you exactly what you need to explore it.

© HarperCollins*Publishers* Limited 2020

10 9 8 7 6 5 4 3 2

ISBN 978-0-00-839717-3

Collins® and COBUILD® are registered trademarks of HarperCollins*Publishers* Limited

www.collins.co.uk/elt

British Library Cataloguing in Publication Data

A catalogue record for this publication is available from the British Library.

Author: Sally Morgan
Illustrator: Rose Wilkinson (Beehive)
Series editor: Rebecca Adlard
Commissioning editor: Zoë Clarke
Publishing manager: Lisa Todd
Product managers: Jennifer Hall and Caroline Green
In-house editor: Alma Puts Keren
Project manager: Emily Hooton
Editor: Matthew Hancock
Proofreaders: Natalie Murray and Michael Lamb
Cover designer: Kevin Robbins
Typesetter: 2Hoots Publishing Services Ltd
Audio produced by id audio, London
Reading guide author: Emma Wilkinson
Production controller: Rachel Weaver
Printed and bound by: GPS Group, Slovenia

Download the audio for this book and a reading guide for parents and teachers at www.collins.co.uk/839717